THE INHERITANCE
AND THE
FATAL VISION

LOIS ROBBINS

Author's Tranquility Press
ATLANTA, GEORGIA

Copyright © 2023 by Lois Robbins

All rights reserved. No part of this publication may be reproduced, distributed, or transmitted in any form or by any means, including photocopying, recording, or other electronic or mechanical methods, without the prior written permission of the publisher, except in the case of brief quotations embodied in critical reviews and certain other noncommercial uses permitted by copyright law. For permission requests, write to the publisher, addressed "Attention: Permissions Coordinator," at the address below.

Lois Robbins/Author's Tranquility Press
3800 Camp Creek Pkwy. SW Bldg. 1400-116 #1255
Atlanta, GA 30331
www.authorstranquilitypress.com

Ordering Information:
Quantity sales. Special discounts are available on quantity purchases by corporations, associations, and others. For details, contact the "Special Sales Department" at the address above.

The Inheritance and The Fatal Vision/Lois Robbins
Paperback: 978-1-960675-40-8
eBook: 978-1-960675-39-2

Inside My Space

This is the story of two lawn boys who are longtime partners from the same picture-perfect Facebook page. Great smiles, great teeth, doing perfectly wonderful social activities, marriages, anniversaries, and birthdays in a sunny beach community.

They had been irreplaceable roommates in college.

There is one problem. They are poor, dirt poor. If they want to provide the perfect backdrop for their storybook page, a hermitage of some kind, they must look to another family for an estate to inherit.

They chose the estate of David Halle, my cousin. The simplicity of the plan was its brilliance. I'm sure they are repeating it now, somewhere, anywhere, anytime.

It's very repeatable.

They forgot one thing, however, someone was watching from heaven. The vision came down from the command center to alarm me of the threat.

CONTENTS

CHAPTER ONE: The Inheritance and the Fatal Vision 7

CHAPTER TWO: The Vision 11

CHAPTER THREE: The Phone Call 14

CHAPTER FOUR: A Tale of Two Cities 20

CHAPTER FIVE: Going to the Trial Per Suggestion 23

CHAPTER SIX: The Contested Case how did it Start 26

CHAPTER SEVEN: A Taste of Heaven 29

CHAPTER EIGHT: My Trial Begins 31

CHAPTER NINE: In my Home at Last 36

CHAPTER TEN: Back to Kentucky 38

CHAPTER ELEVEN: It's The Mail Again 41

CHAPTER TWELVE: Things Heat Up 44

CHAPTER THIRTEEN: A Visit to the Scene of the Crime ... 50

CHAPTER FOURTEEN: I Remember my Family 55

CHAPTER FIFTEEN: I Involve my Son Robert 58

CHAPTER SIXTEEN: The Results of the Investigation 61

CHAPTER SEVENTEEN: My Final Trial 64

CHAPTER EIGHTEEN: The Agreement 67

CHAPTER NINETEEN: The Conclusion 70

CHAPTER TWENTY: The Final Vision 72

CHAPTER ONE

The Inheritance and the Fatal Vision

The Present

Has it been almost ten years? No, eight actually, after some manual mathematical manipulation. A letter just arrived in the post this morning to send my mind crashing back to that fateful evening of the vision that changed things so abruptly in my carefully ordered life.

My name is Angellica Peterson, I am a widowed person living in Sea Isle City and rarely leave my home except for the occasional trip to the grocery store, but I am now entangled in a most complicated lawsuit for the control of an inheritance which I barely had knowledge of.

The letter stated that a set of new lawyers, some names I did not recognize, were ready to settle the case of the estate of David Halle, my cousin. I thought that two years ago we had done just that. Now I remembered that it was a partial payment. They were now prepared to provide the final ten thousand dollars due. No surprise that it's still not settled, they claimed I had not filled out the paperwork properly and sent back the new release and replacement form. I got in my car and passed it on to my new lawyers.

I have heard, with the exception of a selected few, that is what attorneys do best, prevent a case from being settled! I now have the benefit of one of those exceptions, and I can proceed at last to the settlement of this terrible wrongful disaster.

Now, here I was, back again at my kitchen window, looking through the same blue checkered curtains and onto the same woods that performed the strange pageant of the journey that began eight years ago. This was to be a journey that would take me through eight years of legal entanglement and intrigue. It left me confused and exhausted, and strongly convicted that they just barely survived at all.

Before going any further, let me tell you about the four-part vision that, to this day baffles me above my reasons of deduction, to explain. Each occurred briefly, each was eerily silent, and all disappeared as quickly as they appeared. I noticed the faces were never revealed. Each time some sort of filter covered the image that should have been the face.

I was able to decipher the scene only from the surrounding pieces that provided the background setting for each character, or the hairstyles of the prominent figure. Other than myself, no one can authenticate these facts, only someone who has been fortunate enough to have experienced something similar. Surely, our great God performs miracles like this every day for his children.

I had no idea of the significance of the vision at that time. It only became clear after the last meeting I ever had with my attorney, my sadly deficient trial attorney who met with me in the parking lot. He admitted to me sadly, and away from listening devices, that he had been aware for some time of the guilt of the opposition, but was not willing to go any further.

He further glibly passed on the information that the lawn boys in this case had put my cousin's body in a freezer in the funeral parlor the month prior to his viewing. This was to see if any relatives showed up after the obituary they had placed.

It turned out, when at home I consulted an expired calendar, that those four weeks represented the weeks of that four-part vision that I had received at the beginning of this venture. Could it be that someone upstairs was curious about the fact that one of the faithful who was scheduled to appear for his hearing had not done so, and an alert was sent out to see why not?

I guess my attorney was having an attack of guilt about his sad deficiency, or maybe he just needed someone to talk to.

In any case, I don't know why he told me this fact, so late in the case. He must have decided I wasn't very bright, or at least he looked upon me with a rare sympathy now that he'd never have to see me again.

I'll easily agree with that statement, about not being bright. I know now that I took too much time to figure out what was going on.

In any case, those 31 days in the funeral parlor and not in the usual preparation areas gave me my explanation of the timing of the vision. David was in storage in a freezer at the funeral parlor and the visions occurred at the same time.

These powers upstairs were alarmed, and now so was I. I now had my clue about the most unusual apparition of my life.

They must have been busy passing around the news of why this soul passed into eternity with this unusual set of circumstances. It just didn't make sense. Why didn't this just soul go on ahead along the path chosen for his life and be groomed for his assent to his final destiny?

Sure, why not! I was rattled by the above fact. It led to the writing of this story.

Will I ever forget the vision? No, it is etched in my mind permanently. I can go back in time instantly to that evening in my kitchen eight years ago as if it had been this date. What follows is the retelling of that vision.

CHAPTER TWO

The Vision

I love the beginning of spring with the tiny budding of things to come. After the long, chilly shadows of winter, especially this one, narrowly escaping my sister's battle with eternity after a serious stroke, it was good to be home again. My eye was drawn to my kitchen window, which usually followed the cleaning up of the kitchen after dinner, however, a totally unexpected scene met me.

All at once, the woods changed magically into a still shimmering lake of water, no trees or sky, no plants, bridges, an unbroken lake alone, still and quiet. Silver specks appeared in the center of the view as if to draw my attention there; they began to bubble.

As soon as the bubbles appeared, they changed hues, some were pink, orchid, green, or yellow, a great selection of pleasant spring colors, all swirling around in circles.

Suddenly a form emerged, an 8-year-old boy appeared with huge goggles, skinny ribs, and a familiar home-grown crew cut, distinctive with its four corners of peaks sculpted atop a short buzz cut. It was Bobby, my brother performing his favorite sport, diving. I knew it immediately, I had witnessed this event numerous times in my youth in Pt. Pleasant, New Jersey. Bobby looked at me, waved, and slid back down again as quietly as he had appeared. Vision vanished.

Several days passed, and to my great relief, nothing happened. I had had premonitions in the past, impending clutches of doom, followed by a death in the family. Never friends, only family, and now that my family is so small, it is unthinkable.

My short-lived relief ended. It was the following Monday evening. This time, we were back in the fifties, in the back row of the little theater in my hometown. As was the custom, the teen boys who were trying hard to look "bad" smoked in the back row, I could tell, that billows of smoke arose in the back. One head slid up, the same crew cut, only thicker and longer this time, thanks Mom, collar pulled up around his neck, turned, looked at me, and waved. It was Bob again. The vision ended with smoke turning into butterflies and fluttering upwards. They, the butterflies, were outstanding.

One thing was sure, I told myself, time was passing quickly. It was now about nine or ten years later, according to Bob's age. Pretty quick timing for one week's passing.

When the vision ended, this time, I took my sister to see her doctor for a full examination. Fit as a fiddle, he proudly exclaimed, all of the vital organs performing as nature intended. I was bewildered and relieved at the same time. What was going on? I knew something was wrong. This vision was totally different from any experience I'd ever had. Totally different!

I was cautiously apprehensive, I knew this wasn't over, but life as I knew it went on. I checked with my son, and nothing was wrong, my in-laws, again nothing. Relief followed, but not for long. I found myself in this vision at a happy hour, on one of my many visits to his home in the south. I don't know where, but

Bob, hair much more sophisticated, turned from his friends to lift his glass to me. Another Monday evening, this was strange!

I had seen this setting many times as I visited him in Myrtle Beach, South Carolina. He'd say, let's go for some shrimp or oysters, he knew my aversion to drinking, but that's where we would end up. He always had lots of friends, and I knew if I wanted to spend time with him, I'd better go along. Besides, Myrtle Beach has wonderful seafood. I wasn't permitted time with him, he disappeared into the crowd.

This time it ended with champagne bubbles floating upward.

This was followed days later, on a Friday evening, by my last look at him in, the hospital. It is liver bile cancer and spreads very quickly. The vision ended with the view of a coffin, which dramatically rose and diminished in size as it floated upward and disappeared into a cloud of smoke.

At the time of his stay in a Charleston hospital twenty years ago, he had said "Angie, if all these people who've been praying over me cure me, do I have to go the church?" "Yes," I answered, "I'm doomed," he said.

Never fear, dear reader, he made it up to heaven, It was God's plan.

I'd had enough of this speculation and I prepared for a well-earned evening of sleep. As I so often do, I picked up the copy of my current novel, Hamlet, and read forward.

"Stay illusion. If there be any good thing to be done, speak to me"

And so exited the ghost of Hamlet's father

CHAPTER THREE

The Phone Call

I awoke Saturday, the following morning of my last vision, to a new series of demands which would, and still do occupy the fresh reality of a handicapped person in my life. The ordering of a hospital bed, wheelchair, and ramp along with the ordering of agency aids for my sister, Miriam, were at the forefront of my duties at this time. I barely noticed the urgent ringing of the phone.

I had personal turmoil of my own at the time, so the importance of the call didn't take effect on me as it should have.

At the other end of the line, I heard "Are you familiar with the name David Halle"?

"Yes," I responded, "he's my cousin."

"Well, he's dead, I'm sorry".

"You must be his traveling companion", was all I could think to say. I was very aware of his situation, I knew his history well, and I expressed the heartfelt sympathy I had and that I was glad he had shared his end times with a loved one. Dave was a very private person. He had shared his feelings with me of a companion who'd meant a great deal, as he encouraged me to visit Canterbury, England. He'd recently done so, with Eric (the companion he had shared his life with, newly deceased). I felt highly honored that he'd shared such personal news with me.

"I didn't think you'd understand, Angie". Truthfully, the old Angellica wouldn't have".

At this point, I'd like to explain that ours was a telephone relationship, neither one of us liked driving, David and I that is, but the calls went on and on, happily and endlessly talking about our unusual family.

"Hell no", (back in the present) was this caller's response, in this strange phone call. "I simply cut his grass". He suggested that he would never be lowered to such a state and he stated his intentions to me; the purpose of his call. As his lawn man, so he stated, he had finished the lawn and waited for Dave to appear and share a Pepsi with him on the porch, where they normally admired the lawn. He, Dave would then suggest additional work and share some media news.

When Dave did not appear that Saturday, after moving the lawn, Ryan, the name he offered me, checked the door, as the car was in the garage and had been newly washed. When he went inside, he noticed my cousin on the floor and noted that he'd passed away.

He, Dave, had had some internal stomach problems, and, Ryan revealed to me that he had never seen a dead person, went into shock, then home to call his partner.

He called 911 from his home, and now it was just a matter of paperwork.

Ryan had called me because he needed to know the whereabouts of a niece called Luanne, who might be a matter of interest in the settlement. He explained he was helping the attorneys in this case and would do all he could since Dave had become a close friend.

"The funeral is on Monday and I hope to see you there", after giving me the details, he hung up. I now know that he was hoping I'd have no idea where she was, and that was the truth (as I saw it then.)

What a nice young man, I thought, (at the time) to help Dave's lawyers out of pure friendship. I did think it strange that someone so close wasn't aware of how to reach his presumptive heir Luanne.

David had always had such an unusual personality, most people were quite put off by it. We were a theatrical family, it went back to vaudeville. My great-grandparents came over from England for that purpose. I had met elderly folks who had seen them perform in Elizabeth, New Jersey. Dave was the only one left who took up the mantle.

He performed in summer stock in his youth. I witnessed him in "High Button Shoes" in my high school days, a great theatrical talent, I thought. He was in his twenties.

I can still bring up at will, his favorite impersonation of the Bard. It was Puck, laughing darkly at human foibles "Lord, what fools these mortals be." It summed up his view of life. He could command a crowd at will and I'll never forget his deep-throaty laugh, he enjoyed life. I wish it could have been longer.

Upon reflection, as I sat down at my desk to order flowers, I realized that the vision I'd experienced had more to it than I first expected.

I knew now why Bob, my brother, had come to me at age eight, in the vision, when I was six, for that was when we had come to know our cousin Dave. Our Mom and Dad had left us in Point

Pleasant while they built Dad's business and our new home in North Jersey. We went to the Baxter Street school together with David. It created a lifetime friendship, which, while the elder family members were alive, we never forgot. Happy memories, a close family of musicians mainly, some of the most talented, wonderful people I'll ever know.

As I sat in my parlor, I was recalling David's face. He hadn't been necessarily handsome, maybe he had that particular look that worked best for acting, like a blank canvas. An actor was what he hoped to be, in any case. When he said, "now is the winter of our discontent" his features would take on the cunning and cruelty of Richard III. For the present, however, he never escaped the role of high school English teacher and his retirement was only in his mind, that beautiful mind.

Back in the past, when I had occasion to visit his home, it was several hours away, I was so happy to see the pictures on his wall of favorite personalities. These were famous theater and music celebrities signed personally to Uncle Jake, Dave's father, and some to David himself. He (Dave) had felt the same way I had. I wasn't surprised to see they were still in their honored spot.

The following Monday evening, worried that the funeral would be poorly attended, I called the funeral parlor and was assured there were many attendees as Dave had been a popular teacher at the local high school. Many students still remembered happily the Shakespearian festivals he was noted for.

I spoke with the funeral attendant, and he was glad to oblige.

"Yes, there were many presents, and your flowers were beautiful, I was surprised he had a cousin, there was also a young bookkeeper who said yes, she knew of you, you were a beneficiary of Dave's". I was part of the paperwork which had been transferred away from the office, and yes, she knew it.

She seemed upset, but otherwise, the funeral was respectful and calm.

I was reviewing a conversation I had had with Dave in the past. He had expressed a wish that I visit Canterbury, our great grandfather's home. I said that I didn't have the means to do so, and he answered he'd see to it that I could do so. This must be the explanation for the 401K that he set up for me. I'd never been informed of it. I suppose it was meant to be a secret surprise. She, however (the young bookkeeper) was acutely aware of it.

My unease was increasingly growing, I was sure something else more sinister was pending.

My premonition was confirmed when the mail began arriving in droves, duplicate packages from two different lawyers. I began the task of reading piles of legal correspondence and I was beginning to see the problem. Ryan, his lawn person, was claiming the entire estate based on the premise of a handwritten will, written with no witnesses present.

The obituary stated there were no known relatives.

I can recall the so-called "hologram" vividly, and still can, it was burned in my brain, and it was so unbelievable. There were three paragraphs, handwritten in a sloppily, drunken way. It contained no legal phrases, except for the last paragraph, which stated this was to be considered his last will and testament. There was a bequest to a college for 200,000 dollars, and the rest to a valued friend, Ryan something illegible, and his partner (inserted obviously afterward). The rest was hard to read. I at first thought it was copied on a slant, but further comparison to the duplicate showed obviously that it was written on a slant. Not something a scholar such as David would do.

There was also an invitation to attend a court hearing in about six months.

I did the only thing I could think of at the time, I put it all in a big box along with an invitation to attend a court hearing in three months and brought it to a local lawyer, Victor. He was very supportive and suggested I attend the trial.

He contacted the lawyer representing the young bookkeeper, named Carolyn, who said she was contesting Ryan's claim, it sounded suspicious. I made plans to attend the trial. My son agreed to drive me, and I fell back into my other hectic plans, doctors, and more building to accommodate a paralyzed sister.

Sammy, my son, and I had a pleasant afternoon and didn't see any irregularities at the time. We never had time to analyze this new situation, we were working on my crossword puzzle. A big mistake, the first of many, unfortunately!

Since I had six months to figure it all out, I once again immersed myself in my present dilemma, what to do with Miriam. The practical side of me once again got the better part. I had to get her ready to move to her new home in Florida.

CHAPTER FOUR

A Tale of Two Cities

This strange group of trials I was currently involved in was very short in span but involved a lot of waiting and stressing. Time was passing slowly, and I spent a large part of my time engrossed in thoughts of the recent past in Doylestown. I had just returned from half a year with my sister who had recently recovered from a near-deadly stroke in Bucks County, Pennsylvania. It was unexpected and she was in a truly bad way. It was touch and go for about three months. Meanwhile, her husband passed away, no one was sure where this was going.

I was living in Miriam's home until I knew which of the many plans should be pursued. All I knew was that she had just listed her home for sale and they were planning to move to Florida, like so many frigid Bucks County residents. There was much to do, visiting the hospital every day to check on her (Miriam's) progress, showing the home recently listed to eager potential buyers, and planning a funeral during one of Bucks County's biggest snow storms.

I was busy. I had to select furniture which I knew nothing about to fill the new home in Florida, which I also knew nothing about. Luckily, I made a good selection, and I was able to rent out the new home for several years through a local rental agent.

The funeral for Michael still chokes me up when I think about it. More than 200 marines stood in line in the snow for hours, waiting outside out of respect for Mike's service during the Gulf war. I hadn't planned for this large crowd, perhaps ten or twenty marines, but no more. Miriam had just been told about it. She'd been passing in and out of a state of unconsciousness and had to be carefully wheeled in from the ambulance which had so carefully delivered her through the back. It was so tragic, I still grieve for that sad sight that met mine.

I was to remain in Doylestown for seven more months. Very little progress was made in my sister's recovery. I sold Miriam's split level and found a nursing home for her in Delaware. I was ready now to go home at last! I had little time for chats with David.

Meanwhile, in another state, New Jersey specifically, my cousin David was making plans for his own funeral, though he was sadly unaware of it. In the little shore town of Colts Neck, during the Christmas season of the same year, a party was being planned. It would be a holiday party of unusual proportions, complete with presents (imported bourbon and three glasses) stacks of brokerage forms for transfer of portfolio, life insurance, and several pens, in case one wasn't working.

Were there mistletoe, candy canes, and boughs of holly? I don't think so. I didn't fit the script.

Dave's big mistake had been to join the library association, where a father described an unusual new member, elderly, and with very few friends, to his son. Ryan, one of his sons, made plans to meet with him and impress him with his landscaping skills. This was told to me sometime later by a private investigator which I finally had the good sense to hire. And the rest of the story was and still is unwinding.

The two partners intended to cheer him up, this December evening, with an impromptu Christmas party.

It must have been a "late nighter" if this sloppily written note was any indication. I imagine the boys got their handwritten note finished to their specification, reminded Dave of his loyalty to his old college days, and forked over the remainder of his estate to be safely packed away until needed. Of course, they reminded him that they alone had cared about the maintenance of his law and his choice of shrubs.

The only chore left was to remove the dirty glasses and find a safe place at home to hide their clever new missile.

It didn't take much imagination, I needed only to remind myself of Mr. Buotno's trial performance. He had stated there was no record of any legal paperwork regarding property transfers to the boys that usually occurred after such a generous transfer of wealth. The logical mind wonders if Dave was aware of his new will at all!

I seriously do not believe so.

"The fault, dear Brutus, is not in our stars, but in ourselves, that we are underling"

CHAPTER FIVE

Going to the Trial Per Suggestion

I sat in the visitor's section.

I attended the trial as Victor suggested. I was eager to meet the nice young man, who'd appeared so sincere, and to be sure, I was not disappointed. So genuinely glad we were able to make the court case, he'd so looked forward to meeting me, honest youthful blue eyes, searching for my approval. I know now what a successful con artist looks like. He had an honest face, for sure, eager to be of help. He looked me directly in the eyes and stood his ground. Let's get this unpleasantness finished, he suggested. I was completely taken in.

His partner, however, stared at me and ran to the back of the parking lot. I could not understand why, but he looked like a bouncer in a nightclub. Very short, one gold earring, shaved head, attired completely in black leather. Most sinister indeed!

Why should he be afraid of a frail, middle-aged lady in a simple cloth coat of pale blue wool? He had the better instincts, I think he recognized the Sunday school teacher in me. He'd probably been put in the hall more than once. How could two brothers, if they were brothers, appear so unlike one another, yet engage together in a prolonged suit?

I realized that I didn't know much about these two young men, only that one of them was truly frightened. I was to find out later on why when I discovered his true identity.

I thought at the time he recognized in me a person who was not easy to dismiss, I only think so, I'm not really sure. This has occurred more than once throughout my lifetime.

The trial was long and confusing. I just didn't know enough about what was going on, but we were no different from the other unfortunate cases of potential heirs who had been in line for years waiting for small amounts due them from the deceased. The small amounts warded were probably never enough to cover the legal fees built up during the trials.

At the time I was sure that this was the right scenario for my case. Dave had been a school teacher all his life. Apparently, something had been going on that I knew nothing about. This person, Eric, his traveling companion, must have awarded him the large life insurance policy that made up the bulk of his estate, for it was larger than I thought it to be.

I did get to meet with Carolyn who introduced me to an associated attorney who is "a bulldog, he'll get you what you want". I engaged him to make my case for me. The courts would no longer continue with Carolyn's young bookkeeper as she was not related to the deceased. I sure do wish I could have retained Carolyn when I look back in regret.

The case was stacked against her, so I agreed to take on these lawn boys myself.

Per Carolyn's suggestion, I met with my new attorney who promptly relieved me of twenty-five hundred dollars, and another twenty-five a month later, the incorrigible Mr. Buotno he was called, His short round body did not instill confidence. I could not have found a worse lawyer.

Apart from overcharging me, I can't think of another thing he did for my case, except to say, "We'll just have to wait and see". And that's what I did, I waited and waited, but I saw nothing until it was too late.

He was short and round and had a sagging chin, his only resemblance to a bulldog.

I was doomed, and by now I knew it.

This was the beginning of my comparison to that poor usurped king-to-be, Hamlet. I was sure that my cousin had he lived, would have agreed wholeheartedly! His entire family, as with mine, was taken in by the clever slight to hand that occurred.

CHAPTER SIX

The Contested Case how did it Start

One day, the small brokerage firm in a small shore town in North Jersey received quite a shock. Doris, the office manager, made a quick after-Christmas visit to check the mail and fax machines. Something very much unexpected was seated in the fax machine. There was a transmittal requesting that the portfolio of one of their oldest and most loyal clients be sent out immediately. It was far from a giant account and went to an unrecognizable international firm. The name of the firm was not familiar, but it had a valid address.

Doris didn't send it out right away, she'd check with the owners.

It was owned by a retired teacher who'd lived some forty years in the town.

Doris pondered that he hadn't seemed disappointed in them, as she'd recently processed some transactions for him. Something involving his cousin was all she could imagine.

Perhaps he was moving abroad, he did travel frequently in the past.

Dave was by all accounts quiet and always had been. He had lived with both parents in the same home for years and was scholarly and even a little shy. His pension seemed adequate to service his lifestyle and that was all anyone knew.

No, nothing unusual happened at that small brokerage and they were soon busy with other activities. The portfolio was sent out and they resumed their life as usual.

Things were occurring, just not things that ordinary people were subjected to. Things that were happening in the dark of night, things that go bump in the night.

I wasn't there. I can only put together this scenario based on what did happen, and by reviewing the correspondences that were sent to me in droves.

Two years later, as Doris was reviewing the obituaries of the week which she habitually did, a name jumped out in front of her, David Halle, their former client.

It stated that he'd died alone at home after a long illness and that no relatives were living. The funeral would be Monday. She had liked David, she'd attend.

It was a surprisingly lavish affair, well attended. Like most of the visitors, she reviewed the flowers on the wall. One attractive white and pink arrangement caught her eye. It was sent lovingly by a cousin Angie.

Wasn't that the recipient of the small trust she'd so carefully prepared for David? He'd wanted it to be a pleasant surprise, but it had been sent out along with the rest. She, his cousin, surely hadn't died. Who'd sent these flowers?

Two young men in attendance seemed to be controlling the show and seemed proud of the presentation being put on for Dave. Who were they?

Doris approached the funeral director. All he could say was that they had ordered the funeral, and were responsible for all the payments and burial.

Something strange was going on. She'd go to the county court this week. These two boys hadn't been part of his life up until now, and they were in control. They were his landscapers.

Caveat Against the Probate of Will "I Ryan. . .protest against admitting to probate the aforesaid will of 1981. . .unless the terms of same are modified by the aforesaid holographic revision dated. . ."

The lawn boys were admitting their own handwritten will which they had submitted to the court.

We'll just see about that, said Doris to herself. They'd lied in the obituary, or someone had, and to what purpose.

She proposed to consult her friend Carolyn, a trial lawyer.

CHAPTER SEVEN

A Taste of Heaven

This was not the first time in my life I had experienced a vision from above. I need to go back in time to my life in Bucks County.

What a great God we have! He can create a world and at the same time care for His least significant child. His heart breaks when one of His Little Ones hurts or experiences an injustice.

I miss the fifties. Life was so simple. We had a president everyone liked, who didn't like "Ike", as he was called? There were no terrorists, only a cold war threat, and no one knew what that meant anyway (except we took drills in school for such an unlikely event.) I didn't even know that there were two political parties.

In my personal life, there was my family, who would always be there, especially my grandmother.

Everyone should have a person in life who spoils them. In mine, it was my grandmother. She had the talent to see possibilities in me that no one else saw. "Angie, you come from a long line of old maids, do everything possible to change course." Indeed, she taught me how to lighten hair, and use makeup and razors, amid much uproar and she saved copies of "Modern Romance" (highlighted to save reading time).

She died in my senior year of college; she'd even provided some financing. It was an awful year. Luckily, I was pinned to the love of my life and soon-to-be husband, my soul mate. Jim and I had no need of friends, we were our own best company.

I was soon married, and we had our son, the split level, the dog, and the station wagon. Jim had been promoted in his job with the Navy and he was teaching me computers, a true act of love. We had just settled into our new home in Bucks County.

Our son was in the 4th grade. We were expecting a visit from Aunt Dorothy to see our new home in the country. As my son Sammy set the table he was repeating, "The theory of relativity. Relatives will visit". I remember it well.

Dorothy was her beautiful self. She was healthy and happy and loved our new home. We had our last great visit together, though she complained of pain in her left arm. It wasn't major, though.

That night I had my first vision, it was Gran and she was busy sweeping out a room in heaven. She was happy. "Dorothy is coming up here to stay and by the way, you're going to have a baby!" I had never experienced a vision before this. I told no one as—was this really possible?

It could not be so, but Dorothy's funeral followed in three days.

Four years later, the same thing happened except Dorothy was sweeping the same floor, instead of Gran. Bob, my brother was coming up soon and she had to prepare for him. It was the same room, very small, with the same oak paneling. No baby this time. In both visions, they were extremely happy!

Heaven must be wonderful. In the visions to follow, there was no sign of happiness, and they occurred outside of the gates of heaven.

CHAPTER EIGHT

My Trial Begins

It was late June and seemed the perfect time of year for a barbecue for my son's family and that was the only thing on my mind. I wish I'd been involved more with the trial I was now preparing for, the first trial that I was to be actively engaged in.

The evening before my trial I sat in my small living room in my usual tan robe. Once again, my mind was seeing my cousin David, and the baronial presence he left his audience with. Ryan, David's lawn person, seemed more likely to be one of his thespian acquaintances than an actual lawn grunt.

At this moment the student in me, which has never left me since my college days, told me that it was time to prepare myself for the next day's ordeal. I dragged out my legal gear.

As I stirred my steaming mug of tea, I looked back to my last meeting in my new lawyer's office in a kind of reverie.

He had kindly offered the use of his clerk, Maria, to my son and me to organize both sets of papers, which I foolishly agreed to. He looked at me with judicial kindness and seemed interested in streamlining my life to help both of us. Both my son and I agreed things were going well. Everything would have been so different if only, but, oh well, it was probably meant to be.

I brought one of the two evenly stacked sets of papers home and never looked at it until this evening. I had left the other set of papers with him, a big mistake.

My first thought was, where was that strange copy of the handwritten note, that drunken note that was the only basis for inheritance between my cousin and his lawn boys. It was completely gone. It had been left out of the pile of legal papers returned to me, whether deliberate or not, I did not know. They surely were sorted in clean order.

For the first time, the lingering doubt that had been lying under the surface of my skin rose straight to the surface.

If there was any doubt at all that forces were in play in celestial places, I had only to look out of the window. In the darkening skies above, the protagonists in this sinister play were marking their territory with flashes of silver accented by close intervals of roaring thunder and rain pouring against my window.

I drew my drapes and went upstairs to bed.

Now let me take the chance to explain my situation. I would have normally included my son and asked his excellent advice about my doubts, but the optimist in me won out.

I still believed optimistically in the accidental disappearance of the original copy of the homemade will.

I have not explained that my son was a pastor to my new attorney. No question of morality was entered into the case, yet I now wished Sam had looked more threatening.

At the trial, which occurred the next day, the judge entered the small hall. After about the third hearing, the judge summoned my small group. She looked straight at me and said "What are you doing in my courtroom". I answered immediately, "I'm Dave's cousin and he had always said that his niece had been intended as an heir of his estate. She is nowhere mentioned at all in this note".

Judge Judy pounced on this like a tiger "Does anyone here know where she is? You", looking straight at me, "I could find out, I'm sure of where her family lives". She quickly ranted "Everybody out and don't come back until you find her!" We all left.

She grabbed her robes with indignation and took off like a cat in heat. Luckily, she knew better than to try making a decision at that time.

I knew I could never forget that happy summer spent in the woods of Kentucky with my grandmother and the Where family, such wonderful, down-home folks. I must admit, my most immediate memory was of that outhouse, and the many steps that lead to it.

"Back to the present, Angie". I willed myself back to New Jersey!

After the trial, we all headed outside and we met once again in the parking lot. Ryan turned and said "So good to see you again".

He appeared so trusting and sincere looking, I could see what Dave saw in him. The kind of person you would buy insurance or stocks from, the person who had your best interests in mind. This was a tall, slender, sandy-haired man with an easy smile, an attractive presentation to be sure. Something however was wrong. It bothered me throughout the entire trial.

Ryan was either too slick or maybe just a little too professional for a hard-working lawn person. He was also a lot more fragile than my group of hefty lawn people were!

After I retrieved my car, and the relief that passed at doing so, my first thought was, is this the normal reaction of a person who's trying to secure the entire inheritance of one of his lawn clients? This client had indeed passed away alone in his home and with no witnesses present. The only proof of the transference of this estate remained hidden in an informally written note, a strange note hand carried by two Lawn Boys (who possessed the only key to his home).

Very strange indeed! One would think by looking at it, that much partying had gone on in preparation for it.

Thankfully a friend had driven the three-hour trip from my home to the courthouse, and I didn't have to drive home. There were too many questions and too few answers to think about. JoAnne and I discussed anything but the case, we talked about my sister and the tragic state she found herself in, and I as well.

Who were these two boys? Why had my cousin never mentioned them in any of our conversations? Why had Ryan just offered the news that it had taken six hours to make a simple call to 911? He must have thought I had read the police report. I had not. What strange attack of guilt made him feel he had to justify this long delay?

"I just couldn't find my partner anywhere when I went home, and I never make a move without him," Ryan had said. So much for the strong confident lawn person who claimed to be my cousin's only support. This justification might have worked on a twelve-year-old! I have to admit that it did work on me as well.

Perhaps, he was wandering through Dave's study trying to destroy any other wills that may have been in place.

Perhaps, on the other hand, Dave was still grasping for breath.

I used the occasion to tell my new lawyer that he had neglected to enclose the draft of the handwritten note that the three men had made in Dave's home at Christmas time.

"Oh, no problem, I'll send you a new one" Mr. Boutno (my lawyer) had said. "Don't worry, Angie, we'll get 'em". Well, he didn't but I did! He never sent that new replacement either!

This draft never did mention Luanne. Judge Judy had known there was more to this story than there appeared to be on the surface and so did I!

The other will that had appeared along with this hastily written note was a legally written one made several years prior that had named Dave's mother as beneficiary. It had been enclosed with the new document. She had passed away and there were no other relatives mentioned.

CHAPTER NINE

In my Home at Last

We were in the car on the long drive home.

I had loved Dave's mother, she did kind things, especially handing down stylish dresses (we were both small, but my dresses were handmade). I knew that one of the things Dave especially loved about Luanne was that she looked exactly like his mother, with brunette curls and an elfish look about her, quite pretty actually.

I miss the fifties. None of my friends knew of the word divorce. On reflection, none of their parents seemed to like each other. David and my father were no exception, except their wives didn't like each other either.

That was why our families didn't see much of each other, except at the jam sessions the males of the family held. They were wonderful, sweet sounds. The guitar, piano, sax, and drums all danced together with that moody blues sound of forties jazz. Ah, the sound of Bourbon Street in my own home! No one can ever take that away.

I had a copy of "Skylark" made from one of their seventy-eights, but I wore it out. I should have paid more to have the CD made.

Enough memories!

The morning after returning home, I promptly called Mr. Buotno's office to remind him that he had forgotten to include my handwritten will with the other papers. I dismissed in my mind this simple request since he told me it would be easy to furnish, and that I had paid five thousand dollars for the privilege.

It was only when, within the week of receipt of his return envelope, I had the shock of my life. The reply in my hand contained a completely different handwritten hologram complete with legal terminology and composed by someone who was in a very sober frame of mind, someone who had access to great handwriting skills. Gone were the beautiful gothic capital letters used by my cousin that he used to love to show off.

Only the December date was the same!

I quickly went to the phone and called Mr. Buotno's office. I will never forget his response. "Well, do you have the original to compare it with?"

I refrained from reminding him that he was the reason I didn't have it.

I was dealing with the devil and now I knew it. Time to think of alternatives!

I looked beside the chair in my parlor to the large, empty lounge chair beside me with the empty table beside it which should have had a New York Times and worn glasses on the surface. "Speak to me Rob", though I knew he wouldn't.

It was up to me to carry on this battle alone, but was I really alone?

"Now is the winter of our discontent!" rose to my soul from some source within.

CHAPTER TEN

Back to Kentucky

At home after the trial early in the evening, I hit the computer and went online with a surge of activity. I knew the city in Kentucky where Luanne's mom had met her dad Jon, and Dave's only brother.

He, my other cousin, Jon, married a local homecoming queen. She was very sweet, from a small farming family of good old-fashioned Bible-believing Baptists. I loved their old homespun ways. There was a GI bill and a Ph.D. to follow. Much traveling occurred in a small trailer when to the family's surprise (but not mine) Jon took off with a very healthy young cheerleader.

This was not a very good reward for 16 years of faithful companionship to a young college professor. Apparently, sweet and faithful were not what was needed in his life at the time. Jon headed back to the east coast, new wife in tow.

A divorce followed (of the whole southern family apparently), and Jon started a new family in New Jersey.

Several years after the new wife had arrived in New Jersey I was to meet her, this new wife.

Jon and I renewed our old relationship, but she seemed very strange to me. She was loud, boisterous and quickly got a job as a prison warden, (which suited her). She swore like a stevedore and bragged about her straight "A" average in history. Knowing Jon, I was sure it was true. I will not repeat the tasteless remarks he'd often made about his female students who'd regularly made an "easy A" in his class, and the state of their drawers at the time. He was nothing if not honest.

Luckily, they moved miles away, so it never presented a problem. We met infrequently. David refused to meet them at all.

Jon's in-laws in Live Oaks cut off all of my phone requests after the trial. They circled the wagons and let me know this family cared nothing about Luanne's family on the East Coast. I could hardly blame them. I did manage to get through to an elderly gentleman through the internet who wasn't aware that I was being shunned by the family, and was told that Ginanne, Luanne's mother, had passed away from cancer.

I felt so bad. We were close in age (Ginanne and I). We spent quite a bit of time together in my teens. She loved the boardwalk and was lots of fun. I remember her homespun skirts made from bags of flowers. I'd never heard of such things. Following her divorce, she went back to the green hills of the south with her daughter.

After her mother's death, Luanne left for somewhere on the west coast. I didn't know where (my charm is indeed limited!) The one elderly gentleman who would speak with me was now under house arrest.

God loves the Family so much, it was where he planned His children to be raised and nurtured. It must grieve Him when we treat our families like disposable linen to be tossed out with the current mood.

I love to read about the 12 tribes, they are far from perfect people, but they are families.

David never saw his brother again. Things might have been different if they had reconciled. On reflection, why did I feel so bad?

I had tried my best to reconcile them, didn't I?

It took a series of bad circumstances to jar my mind into what was wrong. My wheelchair ramp had fallen apart and I had this fake will to contend with.

Why was it that no one but me noticed the lack of ostentatious gothic scrollwork that David loved to use, in his own Shakespearean way?

CHAPTER ELEVEN

It's The Mail Again

Once again, the mail began arriving in droves, but all from one source this time, from their lawyer via my lawyer. Mr. Buotno kept passing each piece of dubious drivel on to me.

I quit reading it. It contained endless character assassinations about me. I hardly recognized this awful person these missiles described.

There is something good about leading the life of a Sunday school teacher, (I was not one at this time, but I had been one and I knew how to walk in obedience to God's will). It must have been very frustrating for these young lawyers, they couldn't find anything but a stop sign infringement in 1975. They did however pull out of the air the character of the most abusive gold digger of the 20th century! Was that me?

Affidavits, I think they called them, how I had neglected to visit Dave in the hospital, and how by contrast they visited him every day. I found out later on what the estate was worth, well after the case was settled. It was no wonder they spent so much time there.

I had no interest in Dave's money, I was pursuing this case for Luanne, but that was beyond their comprehension. In any case, they had not notified me of his hospitalization, by choice, I think.

Our's (David's and mine) was a telephone friendship, as I mentioned. We never passed on bad news, we gossiped fondly about loved ones.

Dave was extremely vain, he had gained weight and lost hair. He wanted me to think of him as the graying but stately actor who would soon be discovered by the media.

He and I had endless fun discussing our many old maid aunts, especially Aunt Fan. She doted on him especially and had a beautiful sense of humor. She lived to be 100 and lived on grapefruit and wheat germ. The carrots are at 3:00, not to be left out!

In any case that was what David missed talking about. No one but an intimate family member would enjoy discussing these simple things.

Something to think about, and I often do.

Another packet contained more relatives that Dave never knew and wouldn't have cared about in any case. You see I knew the facts of his life as they did not. They were merely doing what they knew or thought they knew would upset me. The more the merrier for my thinking, and better than what the contents of this hologram will suggest. If they knew me better, they could have settled this estate a lot sooner.

Their lawyers, I assume, had their own agenda! The boys replaced them at the very end, I noticed. They were learning as they went along, as was I, the cost of verbal garbage.

A proposal was made to offer each relative 12% of the booty, but the heirs either never took the bait or, as I suspect, they never received the proposal, it was merely meant to discourage me. My cousin Jon had passed on, and his wife had not notified me, but I knew for sure she would have followed up on a request to pursue an inheritance. Did she receive and ignore an offer to get involved in an inheritance from her late husband's brother?

What a miracle! My lawyer finally responded to one of my messages, mostly to tell me he needed another couple thousand dollars. "They have us over a barrel, can't you see that?"

No, I didn't see it at all, the barrel or his need for more money. I reminded him that it was a forged document that they were now circulating. He boldly answered once again, "Well do you have the original"?

I knew someone who did have the original. Carolyn, the lawyer who had sent me the entire packet, to begin with, wasn't returning my calls. "Wasn't this strange?" I said.

She must be busy, was her assistant's reply. She stayed out of the office for a few weeks.

I sat down to ponder the new wrinkles in this strange case.

It was probably a good thing I hadn't hired Carolyn. Was Mr. Buotno worthy of such loyal allegiance, or was he more influential in Colts Neck than I had thought?

Where should I go from here?

This was the time to take my good advice. But sadly, I did not.

CHAPTER TWELVE

Things Heat Up

Some time had passed since the vision that brought me face to face with the nasty trial, I was involved in concerning my cousin David's estate. I was in a wait state again and very discouraged over my lawyer's inactivity.

I could not forget the first of the visions when we were all about seven or eight years old. My brother Bobby and I were living in Point Pleasant, a beautiful time in childhood.

We had no time for problems, such as why in the world we were there at all.

David even at that early age had the genes of Julius Caesar. He had come up with a crown somewhere and had a long plaid scarf on hand, as well as a sword, should he ever win one of our many bouts of King of the Hill. Bobby and I would let him win once or twice in sympathy and try to keep a straight face as he thundered his victory speech. What a masterful command of the Roman military machine.

"Beware the Ides of March", ominous, yes?

Suddenly the hounds of heaven made their appearance to stir things up and bring me sharply back to the present. A piercing truth destroyed my confidence in the phrase, "justice for all."

There were two separate hologram wills circulating, and no one but me was aware of the fact.

When on the event of the next trial with Mr. Buotno, I was told I was not needed, my spine drew up in self-defense mode. These were the non-vested items, which I was not part of.

"Well, I used to be", I thought! They would be discussing the former 401K that had been changed and sent out to a new brokerage, per the paperwork I was newly the recipient of.

I couldn't read the copies, they were so blurred. I now believe it was intentional.

Non-probate elements were being discussed, Mr. Buotno explained. "It doesn't concern you." I thought to myself as I quietly sat in the back row, it was probably a good thing I ignored my lawyer's request that I not attend.

Mr. Boutno caught my eye and started showing off for my benefit. How do I know? He never carried out the plan he expressed. In outrage, he accused the opposition of taking advantage of a lonely old man, as no activity had occurred, no attempt to legitimize the note or transfer of property which usually happened. He's seen it often, he said.

Laurence Buotno was spectacular. He swung to the right, then to the left in disbelief and outrage.

He had a great possibility, I thought (at that time).

How lucky could I be!

However, this one evening of generosity seemed to have never happened again and was promptly ignored. The now new contestants, the friends of my cousin Dave, were here on after in the driver's seat.

Yet, a nagging doubt formed in the back of my mind. This man seemed to have a split personality. He moved in and out of inaction like a chameleon.

While Mom was alive, I had come to like and respect her attorney, Ray, very much. He found her amusing (people either loved or hated her, I loved her, she taught me how to get along with difficult people at an early age). He told me that he always found us laughing together when he walked in on us in his reception area. Once, in her raincoat, she found two hundred dollars. I promptly told her to put it on the collection plate the next day. "Nonsense", she replied, "it doesn't cost anything to pray, they don't need the money." As he walked in, he laughed with us.

Sadly, he had retired recently to Maryland.

I thought fondly of the past we had shared.

Ray steered me through a very difficult "season" in my life and made the path easier for a possibly difficult and stressful transition. I handled her estate for her, and Ray made it easy for me. I called him. He asked me if my lawyer had indeed shared his "plan" with me and had ever shared his knowledge of the opposition's strengths and weaknesses. "No" was my easy answer. No, we had never discussed a plan at all!

It might be time for a change. That fake hologram was stuck in my mind in a way that wouldn't quit.

He suggested I meet with a young, newly graduated lawyer, whom he had hired for his office and admired, named Donella. I did as he suggested. I met her and liked her very much. I sent a letter of dismissal to Mr. Boutno, as was required. We were planning to appear in court again, but I hadn't finalized the paperwork with Donella, the travel distance was just too great. I regret that decision so much.

The third court case was about to begin. It was the third court appearance I had experienced in my life and was indeed the strangest!

On the occasion of the third trial, Mr. Buotno was not there, as I expected. When it came time to appear before the judge, I said "Your Honor, I've had to dismiss my attorney".

Just then, his large body came barreling through the door and to the front. It was the most activity I had witnessed in him.

The Judge said regally, "Will you two take your differences out in the hall and don't return until you've settled them!" instead of, "we're proceeding without you". I certainly jumped at her instructions. I wonder what would have happened if Donella had been there. She certainly wouldn't have jumped to attention on command.

I have since discovered that dismissing your lawyer in a court of law is allowed.

I think every law that could have been broken indeed was broken in this case!

We did as instructed.

"Angie," he said outside, "I thought you liked me. I never received any letter from you.

(After I explained that I had severed our relationship by mail.) I want to help you so much—give me a chance to prove it! Let me get you through today at least." I caved! I bought it, a hook, line, and sinker. I thought I was seeing honest sweat on his forehead.

He made me feel that I had been a great disappointment and had caused much distress in his life.

I sincerely hope that I did.

I sent the letter on my computer to Donella, with much regret. I still feel that nothing short of complete justice would have satisfied her, the aggression showed in her eyes. I did not want to send my cousin's two best friends to jail. Not bright on my part!

In all honesty, a friend of much-practiced law later told me I did the right thing. It would have cost more time and money and would have not added to my cause. Satisfaction is a short-lived thrill. Prolonging this trial would only have cost more money.

Mr. Buotno had explained that I was the only one separating those two criminals from their dreams of a lifetime, my cousin's estate.

I truly believed him, at the time. As soon as he was assured, I was back in his ball court, he reverted to his previous strategy of "we'll just have to wait and see."

Jon's first wife had lost out on every count. I still think of her so fondly, that cute southern drawl, so full of fun. No lawn boy would have separated her from her daughter's inheritance. Had she lived things might have been different.

David never saw his brother again when he found out about his remarriage. How I hoped they would have reconciled. On reflection, why did I feel so bad?

I had tried to reunite the two of them, but it didn't work out. I was told to stay away from their business. I did so.

I come from a very stubborn family. It's one of our most obvious traits. Still, it kept me involved in this strange case.

This once hopeful family was so full of talent, and we'd had it taken away from us!

Alas, as had the young lord Hamlet! At this point I so wished I had the talents of the great Bard, he wouldn't have stood quietly by and given in to an overbearing lawyer.

CHAPTER THIRTEEN

A Visit to the Scene of the Crime

The case of the Estate of David Halle was finally picking up steam. After a year of requests, I was allowed to visit my cousin's home which, despite protest, was still not secured, but was being "protected" by these dubious landscapers. (I was to be told much later they had only two clients).

It was a small rancher, but I hardly recognized it when I drove up. It had a million dollars worth of landscaping surrounding it!

Dave was the actor in the family. He did summer stock throughout college. He had that flair for being center stage when he walked into a room. I found it amusing and enjoyed his visits immensely.

David had settled down when he finished college.

I, on the other hand, went to college by force. "Dad, they loved me in Pride and Prejudice" would not budge my father at all.

I did not need acting lessons, was his final verdict. There was quite a stir in my family when, instead of applying for college, I set up a team of acting and voice coaches in New York City instead. These coaches insured my theatrical failure by sending a huge bill to my dad. Now I am no longer naïve about the value of a huge check in the business world.

Perhaps my brief theatrical background could help to unwind this strange story of the two incongruous lawn workers and their ambitions. It was worth a try. It was a family trait.

So, when the time came for the visit to the family estate of David Halle, I put into effect the best plan of action I could think of. I made the decision to go with the easiest and most successful of 'my acts', the incredibly dumb blond.

The time for being accommodating to the ringleaders of this case of fraud and deception was passed. I wasn't sure who they were specifically, but it didn't matter, they were all beneath contempt for me.

The cloud around this story was beginning to clear, but in my defense, I was busy with my new mystery. It was taking all my time, and I was prepared.

So, when the aging but dumb blond met the administrator at Dave's house, he faced my innocent pink outfit and quite an out-of-date hat. I asked "is there an ocean around here? How nice!" He looked into my questionably vague eyes.

"You haven't been here recently?"

I just looked at him, and said absent-mindedly, "I don't remember at all. It's all so confusing".

He looked at me warily, as if to say, "What are we stuck with now?"

He then reminded me that rules of conduct would not allow him to converse with me about anything involved in the case at all.

This was a practice called for my later performance as I saw it. It might be too late for practice, however.

I was finally aware of what I was up against, and it wasn't pleasant.

Grace and I were accompanied by the newly assigned

administrator and encouraged to bring a camera, which I do not know. All of David's priceless collection of sixteenth-century Chinese and Japanese memorabilia had been removed, and some of his paintings as well. His obsession with rare manuscripts of the sixteenth century had never paid off. His collection had been magnificent. I did not see them at all. I had no proof, unfortunately.

Dave was an English instructor. He had gotten into his role of Empire a little too enthusiastically and surrounded himself with gorgeous enameled netsuke boxes and Chinese ink stones, all in a study corral he had created to show them off. These were located in his study at the time of my last visit with Mom. The study had the appearance of an English manor.

Once again, I was seeing David. The terrain of that face would shift and he would become Hamlet, musing upon a skull. "Why may not that be the skull of a lawyer? Where be his quiddities now?" His Hamlet was full of fire, his wordplay like the deadly glint of a sword. Like Hamlet, he tended to overthink things, his fatal tendency, and not to reach sensible decisions.

"Oh David, I miss you. I was never able to rise above Jane Austen and that hot Mr. Rochester".

Outside of this study, the home had the aura of a standard development rancher possessed by a bachelor, recently with an obsession for lots of shrubbery.

Mom and I tried in the past to get him to remove his valuables from safer storage, but he stated their value and hung onto them for the comfort they gave him.

It was the way, unfortunately, Dave did most of the things he did! He had no one to whom he had a responsibility. Who am I to judge, anyway?

He'd been alone for a long time. This was just the way he liked things!

There was no one to tell him what to do, how to do it, and when to do so.

When he bragged "You have no idea what these things are worth, Aunt Mary" he was right, she didn't when she suggested he put them away for a while.

There was someone who did know what they were worth.

Someone had a stake in shipping valuables, which someone did, for they were all removed from the house. It explained one of the entries the detective I hired, later on, would expand on.

I took pictures of an empty house. The visit took place one year after the trials, but I noticed it did not have the smell of a comfortably occupied home. There were absolutely no tapes or CDs on the television stand, and it had been recently dusted.

Poor David had been the victim of a chance meeting at a library association meeting by two parasites, who had no business thrusting themselves into the life of a seventy-year-old retired teacher.

He should have been watching his TV peacefully surrounded by the things he loved so much, instead strangers were marching through his estate, looking for things that might be of value. I think we were too late!

All traces of movies had been removed, and the TV console looked so lonely. The same dishes that had been washed lovingly by the family were still there, but they were located unworthily outside of the study. They had been purchased at Sears.

I noticed the presence of taped-up boxes, but I did not have the authority to suggest they be opened for scrutiny.

Someone had removed several books from his office shelves. I wondered if one had been titled "How to Write Your Own Will" and avoid legal fees.

This same someone had put yellow colored water in a urine bottle beside his bed, with no signs of mold or odor after a year, someone who knew nothing of the caretaking of the elderly.

Apparently, the lawn boys had never witnessed mold on urine.

I could have done a much better job, but that was irrelevant.

I returned to south Jersey discouraged once again, but more than ever determined to bring in my son to this investigation. Following the results of my discovery, I believed another visit to the house should have occurred. I had to do something, but what? Once again, my attorney was away on vacation, a rather long one. He took lots of them.

"Oh, God. Horatio, if thou didn't ever hold me in thy heart in this harsh world, draw thy breath in pain and tell my story."

.

CHAPTER FOURTEEN

I Remember my Family

Those family dishes at David's had really stirred memories of family. Stay focused, Angellica.

I especially miss those Thanksgiving, with Aunt Fan who always requested we save the best part of the turkey, the part that jumped over the fence last. David and I could eventually discuss Thanksgiving without that choice tidbit. My grandmother and her sister would laugh endlessly and that was that. Who can forget these family memories indeed?

"Do what you want Angie, my Gran would say, but take her advice and you'll end up alone just like she is, lonely." I have nothing more to add to that! Thank you, Gran, I never ended up alone.

Dear Aunt Fan was almost correct, I did end up alone, but only after a long eventful marriage. On this fact she was right, you never knew where he had his lips last, but oh, I have some wonderful memories to carry to bed late at night.

Gran, I miss you so much. She instilled the sense of independence that has always annoyed so many of my loved ones. I always had a five-dollar bill tucked away somewhere so I could take a train to her home in Pt. Pleasant and get off at the train station where Uncle Mat worked, he would take me to her house. This was in case I should be treated unfairly by my parents. I did it often. She assured me no one at home knew about it. I believe every child should be so lucky.

How did Dad know to pick me up after a day or so?

Had this family still been functioning with the normal activity of birthdays, anniversaries, and the inevitable Thanksgiving (and the laughter and gossip which accompanies them), this intrusion would never have occurred. These intruders would have passed on to another victim.

David had intended to provide for a niece who could use a little help, through an unfortunate happenstance not of her own making. Luanne, your father loved you in his way but was too ill to fight for you at the time.

I miss my family so much. Dave had spent practically all of his life as a hard-working English teacher, respected by his students, providing for his keep. He was responsible for the Shakespearian talent seen in the festivals so heavily attended. I can still see his silver streak across his forehead, his newest addition to his English baron looks, in my mind.

Through our Aunt Fan, I heard all about his rise as a Shakespearian actor in summer stock, whether true or not I do not know. She adored him, the son she had never had.

I also heard about all the eager young playhouse cast members in his English class who would otherwise have been overlooked in this long-forgotten impoverished city.

Somehow, he managed to introduce them to his former theatrical experiences so they could experience the wonderful enthusiasm of a long-forgotten century in a place far, far away.

The crowds the funeral attendant told me about attested to this fact.

I received a call from someone I did not know, who asked me if I knew what the last play was that David had been in.

"High Button Show" I answered. "You're the one I'm looking for" was his answer!

How could I forget? David talked about it all the time.

CHAPTER FIFTEEN

I Involve my Son Robert

Sammy was surprised I hadn't notified him sooner. We made immediate plans to meet. After a long session at his home, we found a private investigator, Charlie, and assembled the literature he would need. We collated, copied, and faxed all evening. Sam filled out all Charlie would need.

I took care of the blank forms to describe my family relationship. I didn't take it seriously, now that I knew no one was interested. My lawyer had said that this was so. "Angie, don't spend too much time filling out these forms. You're the only one that cares"

Someone upstairs did, however.

Later that evening I received a call shortly from Charlie, my newly hired private eye, stating that Ryan came from an ideal Facebook family. "I'm sorry I couldn't be more help,"

This was a family, he explained, anyone would be pleased to know including their membership in the Library Association, their marriages, and their lovely children.

In the morning light things were different. The following morning a different message appeared in my email. "Angie, I couldn't sleep all night, something's wrong—I spent the whole night at my computer. Hang on, I'll be in touch". Nothing like this had ever happened to him before. He had been glued to his seat by an unseen power until his eye fell upon a hitherto unseen entry.

Something indeed was wrong. Ryan's brother was not a landscaper at all but had held a license as a broker in the state of Arizona at the time of the writing of the hologram will, and had been fired from his job in June of that fatal year, even though he had been an officer in that company.

That company handled "legally eligible recoveries" and had been registered as a foreign limited liability company, whatever that means.

As of this writing, he no longer had a listing with FINRA, the organization that handled ethics for stock brokers.

In my short career, as a profession, I had been described as an assistant. I still cannot figure out what this company did.

However, since this event, I have tried to get the opinion of others more informed than I, and none of them knew the answer.

I now knew as well why I had not been given any of the particular details of the transfer of the portfolio of David's, what was in it, and where it went. I had only my lawyer's statement at the second trial that everything had occurred at the date of, or within the date of the handwritten will. The copy I had received was so badly smudged, and intentionally so.

I'm sure I would find that the dates of all the documents signed were days after that fateful Christmas celebration. I now knew also that blank transfer forms traveled with pens and paper, (a very easy task to accomplish if one had knowledge of doing so).

Ryan's brother was living in Florida at the time of the writing of this questionable document, and he was involved in the resale of "collectibles" at that time.

Charlie, my investigator, was also working out of Florida at this time. I think that was why he was able also to tell in his report of a court case he (Charlie) had been involved in regarding Ryan's brother. His brother had been dismissed from the firm he was employed with.

This had been the company described in the FINRA file as "convertible distressed receivables" which converted them to cash. I sure do wish I had spent more time on that report. I had moved it upstairs to the attic. Another big mistake.

This was a very boring report to me at the time, though I no longer think so. What items were considered "distressed receivables"? In this strange case, anything was possible.

Was this the final resting place for David's antiques?

It was time for a visit to my broker.

CHAPTER SIXTEEN

The Results of the Investigation

That Harry, Ryan's associate or brother, had looked more like a bouncer than a lawn boy when we first met, and that he ran as if the game was up, suddenly cleared up the mystery in my mind. Now that I knew he hadn't been mowing lawns in many years but had instead been working as a broker for the state of Arizona, the bewildering scene was at last magically explained. It could explain the fifty-yard dash in the parking lot of the courthouse.

It would also explain his guilt, in any number of things I now knew about him.

All at once I knew what the game was, and it took all of my acting ability to get through this case.

I was aware now of the immensity of the job ahead of us. I had thoroughly misjudged the extent of the duplicity of the boy's activity. They were trained experts in deception.

My son Sam had become quite alarmed by these new finds of the investigator, and I felt relief that I had included him in my case.

I was finally aware of what I was up against, and it wasn't pleasant.

Soon I was to find myself in the office of my broker.

"What would you do if?"—I walked into his office with the most bewildered look he'd seen on me. I have him some background information on what I'd been involved in the past year or so, and he was loyally sympathetic. We'd been through a lot of history during the great moves of the market and watched it rise and lower together. I believe Ed thought of me as one of those buy high, sell low, investors.

It's all a game of chance to me, my background is not financial but I can't help but be attracted to it. It's a great game for people with time on their hands, but not too great for one's financial health. In any case, ours was a social relationship.

Ed knew me better than the administrator I'd met at my cousin's home. He'd know I did have a shrewd eye when it was needed. He cautioned me to be careful and gave me the Google info I needed to get a FINRA report on Harry in Arizona.

I went home freshly armed with my new ammunition I promptly got started. I made a phone call to Sammy and asked him over for some of my lemon pie.

"Why are you investigating your broker, Mom?", my son asked before his fingers whizzed through the internet.

"See, look" I answered. On the FINRA web page, it alerts you in bold letters not to enter into any financial contracts with anyone who isn't recommended or filed with them.

"You can never be too sure", I wisely responded.

I then explained what Ed, my broker, had told me of his knowledge of Finra.

He, Ryan's brother Harry, was guilty of all of the warnings. He had never been recommended to me and he was no longer listed with them. He probably was guilty of more than one, if the dealing I'd had with him was any clue, he'd been at it for a while.

He wasn't any longer filed with FINRA, but he used to be, according to Charlie. That meant he was not recommended by them. That was all I needed!

At the time I was in his office, I inquired of Ed whether he had any information about a company that did recoveries of uncollectible inheritances or distressed receivables. He did not.

Neither did anyone else that I knew.

That Ryan's brother had found a company who did this was also in part no surprise at all. I'm sure they as a company had access to many handwriting experts. A good look at their books would have shown records of recent sales of Chinese and Japanese sixteenth-century memorabilia. The information he had access to was sure of great value to this new game of his. Was it perhaps not a new game, but one he had been navigating for years?

I was now ready to face the music at my last and final trial, to be held at my lawyer's office, with court officers in attendance. I put together the investigator's report, perhaps I padded it a little! I think I added my new dryer manual.

I reread the report. I had shown it to Sam. With what I know now, the line I should have followed was to request a delay. I had a more pressing thing to do.

I resurrected my pink suit.

"The plays the thing to raise the conscience of the King."

CHAPTER SEVENTEEN

My Final Trial

It was the morning of what was supposed to be my final inquisition. It was to be informal and to take place in Mr. Buotno's office (so I would feel comfortable).

Why had they thought I needed to be made comfortable? I felt very much at ease.

When I entered Sammy's car in the morning, he couldn't keep the surprise out of his eyes.

My hair had turned blue or grey and I sported a fifties-style straw hat, along with granny glasses.

Sammy and I walked in discussing our excellent breakfast on the boardwalk. What a nice morning, what a view! I was asked why I had brought along someone else - to drive of course.

Our trip included a magnificent view of the ocean, while we engaged in some bolstering conversation designed to keep me from backing down. I was ready to do so.

At the office in Colts Neck, I was directed alone to the ground-floor meeting room set aside for us.

The two lawn boys and their lawyer were across the big table. I was alone on the other side, the court reporter in the middle. She was flirting with one of them. I wanted to tell her what a waste of time that was. They were married. But I behaved!

The opposition started to ask me a question. As we were officially off the record, I waited very demurely as I looked above my granny glasses, and answered that I was unable to reply until the results of my investigation were in. What investigation? I looked down at my notes, pretending to have no knowledge of their meaning. "I've initiated an investigation under FINRA", I said. Just then my attorney grabbed my sleeve and said "Upstairs, right now, Angie".

This was not, however, before I saw their faces, Ryan turn literally green. It really did, you know. He nearly fell off of his confident and arrogant stool.

Upstairs my lawyer said, "You've been holding out on me." He was very angry. This was not the course he was planning. "Let me see that report", and, as he grabbed it out of my hands, it included only the first page of Charlie's report and my new dryer manual. "Where's the rest?" he impudently demanded. Now I knew for sure which side he was playing on. "I forgot it."

"You told me no one cared about the report I filled out and I didn't think it was important."

Suddenly, I was looking into the grey eyes of my son Sammy's skepticism. He on the other hand was looking into a new set of wizened blue eyes, mine.

"I'll go back downstairs", as he glared at me. "What is a FINRA?" "Well, the F is for Federal", I replied.

When he came back upstairs Mr. Buotno came back breathing heavily with an offer of 10,000 cash in tow.

"Add eighty thousand to it," I said, per the instruction of my son.

"They're scared, you've got it" my lawyer muttered, in desperation. He promised to stay with me during my final and most difficult ordeal. So much for his promises!

"Well, I'll go home now and beat the traffic".

My husband had always called me a true daughter of Eve. I thought so at that time.

Looking back, Rob would not have agreed in this case. My husband had been a contract negotiator for the defense department of the Navy. He would have surely said that if the landscaping team had so easily accepted the offer of eighty thousand, they could have been worked up to a much greater sum. I, however, was never as bright as he.

In my defense, you might say, I had given in for a reason. Ray, my mother's retired attorney, had steered me to the only honest employee of the court, as far as he knew, an elderly clerk.

I met him outside of the hearing at my last trial. The elderly and graying individual escorted me to a quiet room where we could talk off guard. I was never told his name. He told me very quietly not to rely too heavily on that sealed document in the archives. "They tend to disappear all the time around here." He turned and disappeared as silently as a cat, probably as well as those sealed documents.

Donella, my briefly secured attorney, and I had tried to get a copy when we went to the archives and were quickly rushed out of the building and told not to come back until they were "unsealed". I wonder if they were there to eat all!

Suddenly a sense of panic invaded my being. I had waited too late to include my son Sam in my trial. All my usual confidence had disappeared. I was not sure I was handling things well, and now I was positive. I was out of my element.

Only one thing I knew for sure, I couldn't wait for us to get home.

CHAPTER EIGHTEEN

The Agreement

When we left for the long ride home, I just didn't care to see any lawn men, brokers, or lawyers for as long as I lived. This horrible episode in my life was over for good. Praise God, over at last!

Halfway home during the ride on the Parkway, we stopped for dinner at a little rest stop.

I treated myself and Sam to a Greek salad. We skipped dessert.

I told him what Mr. Buotno had said as he walked me to my car. "Did you know your cousin Dave was a miser?"

It was the only clue I had to the amount in Dave's estate. We had never discussed dollar figures.

"Mom, why do you suppose he said that? Could it be there was quite a bit more in his estate than you thought? You'd better think about this."

I dismissed this fact from my memory.

My last words were that I would never, ever agree to this fake note. I insisted on waiting for the unsealing of the hologram, and we would proceed from there. I had to admit to myself that this copy he showed to me as I entered his office for the last time, was close to what a court would consider legitimate.

It, the copy, had all the trappings of legal jargon and there was not a whiff of a drunken all-night party to be detected at all about the entire document.

I did my best, to reread that new hologram Mr. Buotno was promoting.

I read it with fresh eyes as he suggested to me. I called him on the phone the next day. "I think it's as good a copy as you'll find. I wish I could agree with you, but I can't" I said.

"Oh, try again". I would do that, but I didn't mean it.

I trusted my memory. I always have.

Although I had stated vehemently the words "never, ever agree" when last we met, I had a nagging thought that we might honestly not get to see this "unsealing" of the aforementioned document, per the "only trustworthy court official" Ray knew of.

I can't forget Ray's friend's words to me. "Mrs. Peterson, don't depend on ever seeing that document. Papers like that tend to disappear forever around here". I had no reason not to believe him.

Why couldn't I take it one step further and demand to see that note?

About that original handwritten note, it was probably shredded by now. Mr. Boutno was nothing if not thorough.

He, of all people, knew the truth about the substitution that had taken place in his office.

He could stick to his fake story, and I couldn't prove it.

I guess that's the kind of thing that makes the legal world go round and round.

Two weeks later I received the agreement in the mail. I was designated the primary heir, per the legal will of 1980 where

David left his entire estate to his mother, receiving 80,000 dollars, the college 100,000, and the two boys received the balance. I signed and returned it to his office after the agreement was reviewed by the judge. I had no idea what the balance was. I blame myself entirely for not finding out.

Yes, I read the entire document. I called Mr. Buotno on the phone. It still says I will personally be responsible for the taxes. "Oh, just sign it. Don't you trust me?"

Exhaustion was my pitiful excuse, but I had a busy life with my sister and just wanted to get back to it. I told you I was never as bright as my husband Rob.

In my final conversation with Mr. Buotno, my attorney, I was NOT told that this was a million-dollar estate. He only repeated that my cousin was a miser and that he had been pursued by these two boys for eight years. This was no surprise to me. He also, in an attack of guilt, told me that the two "boys" had put David in a freezer for a month before the funeral. This was the moment that the meaning behind my vision became clear. I realized, as never before, that I was a central figure of one of God's many miracles!

Once again, the dates matched exactly the dates of my vision.

When I came back down to earth several days later my first thought was of Luanne and how I had failed her. How to complete disgust with the system had gotten the best of me. I could go on and on. Throughout this entire trial, I had a pure dislike of these legal eagles that put us through this.

Peace would follow if there was any justice at all. I received a partial check and a lot to think about. I also had plenty of places to spend it.

CHAPTER NINETEEN

The Conclusion

A crime story is most interesting to the victim. First, the crime was introduced by a vision, making it a true mystery, to me, but not to God. I know now that He is aware of every soul, and that moment when it passes into eternity. He caused a bookkeeper in Red Bank to read an obituary. The rest is history. My history at least!

There were several hours unaccounted for between the time Richard found my cousin and the call to 911. I believe Dave was not dead, he was calling for help. That would explain the return to Richard's home to me. That was what he claimed he did. He said he had to call his brother to see what he should do. I believe he spent the time looking for the fatal note of December 23.

Since the time that the New Jersey Attorney General reviewed my case, any handwritten will not be allowed in court, unless brought before an attorney. I believe I may have been instrumental in causing any such similar tragedy to happen again. It was worth it if that is so. My son told me so.

He surprised me by applauding my efforts in this venture.

"Mom you did this all by yourself, and you did great, but next time, you and Grace had better include me. You could have been hurt, these were hardcore criminals." He had a skeptical look in his eye, I'm just one of those helpful people and this time it was to my cousin, David.

He hadn't seen Harry running from me in the parking lot of the courthouse!

I just know the boys are somewhere in Brazil laughing at all of us poor citizens of New Jersey. That's OK. I just hope I never have to do this again.

I mean it this time.

Woe indeed to us mere mortals.

CHAPTER TWENTY

The Final Vision

I was at peace, at last, no not exactly peace, but resignation. This awful trial, I thought at the time, was indeed over. I could get back to my obscure and simple life.

It was an evening in the fall, and I was sitting on my wicker rocker admiring the hosts. They are at their greatest beauty this time of year, full and healthy, a lovely tribute to the end of summer.

Suddenly the scene in front of me became a still, sandy desert, a Sahara of a sort.

As it stopped in from of me, the bulky figure lifted his hat and made a deep bow toward my porch, a grand theatrical, and sweeping bow. This was David's salute to my success.

Up until now, I wasn't sure how he'd felt about his friend's failure to have his plan thwarted by me. Now I knew for sure and felt justified and relieved at the same time.

Thanks, Dave, see you when I get there!

Something forced my eyes upward. What a magnificent scene in the sky above. The stars were sparkling brilliantly above. Polaris, the North Star was overshadowed by Alpha Centauri in her exuberance. Happiness in the heavens could not be contained this night in this, her grand celebration.

In my mind, the figure in brown was headed upward and growing younger all the time.

"Good night, good night, sweet prince. Flight of angels sing thee to thy rest".